DOUGH KNOT MURDER

CEECEE JAMES

I joked to my husband that I was going to dedicate this book to myself. Why? Very good question! Well each one of my other books (over twenty at the time of this publication) are dedicated to them! <3 And I realized that until another writer comes into the family I might never get a book dedicated to me.

But, in truth, they are my heart. And in dedicating this to them, I am dedicating the story to those who make me the happiest. I want to go on to write something humorous, but I'm just getting to dang sappy to do it. So, without further ado, this is——

For my Family, my favorite Christmas gifts of all. <3

CONTENTS

Blurb   vii

Chapter 1   1
Chapter 2   8
Chapter 3   17
Chapter 4   31
Chapter 5   38
Chapter 6   42
Chapter 7   49
Chapter 8   56
Chapter 9   63
Chapter 10   76

Chapter 11 Recipes   85

BLURB

Dough Knot Murder
   A short story with free recipes

In this Baker Street spin-off, Oscar and Cecelia find themselves along with the guests of the bed-and-breakfast snowed in this Christmas holiday. What should be all sugar cookies and hot cocoa takes a drastic turn when one of the guests turns up cold—as in stone cold dead. With no help in sight, the two hope to find the killer before anyone else gets iced out. Including them.

   I love the Baker Street Series!

   Good mix of characters to keep you turning pages & looking forward to next.

   Reward yourself by making some of the recipes included!!!

   Be sure to read through the end to catch a few special

recipes including Cecelia's Christmas morning bread, a little something from Oscar, and my own secret Chicken Pot Pie! Plus a note from me! This story is special to me (I share a bit more about that at the end), and I hope you love this grumpy, darling man as much as I do! It turns out, the world would be a better place with a few more Oscars and Cecelias.

CHAPTER 1

*T*he clouds in the sky lay across the horizon like a thick, gray, flannel blanket, threatening to ruin the rest of the day with a snow storm. It was not good news to the retired FBI agent who rubbed his arthritic hands together in an attempt to warm them. He blew a plume of mist on his fingers and then stuck them under his armpits.

"Bear!" he yelled, his face getting lost behind another misty cloud. "Bear, get over here!"

The man's name was Oscar. Right about now he was feeling sorry for himself and in a big way. It was too dang cold to be standing out here doing the chilly-willy dance while waiting for that confounded-dog. There she was laughing at him from behind the crab-apple tree, tongue dangling out. He sighed and tried snapping his fingers. They were stiff, and the sound produced was like two pieces of sandpaper being rubbed together. Not only did it irritate him further, it did no good in enticing the animal to come back.

Oscar couldn't believe he was in this predicament. He had just arrived home from spending far too much money at the grocery store—for the price of milk he expected there would be a calf included—when, upon opening his front door, the dog ran out, nearly tripping him in the process.

The beast in question was a defiant, puffy Pomeranian who now dashed toward the bushes in a yellow blur. Mushy piles of leaves and mud, wet from an earlier cold rain, splashed on her underbelly.

"Confound it, Bear! Will you get over here!" Wait. Was she thinking about rolling? Desperately, Oscar tried a new tactic. "I have a treat!" He threw out the last word with as much wheedling as his vocal cords that sounded like a chainsaw could attain.

She sniffed around a pile of rotten crab apples, completely ignoring him. Oscar considered his last, desperate option. His late wife had named her Peanut, and he'd always detested it. The animal seemed in on the joke and never responded to her new name, try as he might.

He might have to resort to calling her Peanut. Even worse, he might have to do it in a sing-song.

A bell happily jingled from her jaunty red collar, causing the grizzled man's eyebrows to lower even more. How had that gotten around her neck? He definitely would never do anything that silly.

"What is that you have Has someone gussied you up, you little tumbleweed?" His eyebrows trembled like an avalanche about to fall.

Behind him, soft footsteps came down the hall. "What are you grumbling about, Oscar?" A woman appearing close to his age poked her head out the front door, her white hair piled high in a bun. Her name was Cecelia, and she ran the bed-and-breakfast next door. She calmly wiped her hands on a dish towel, the corner of her mouth hinting at a smile. "I see you're back, already. Did you get my ginger?"

"What have you done to Bear?" Oscar asked, pointing indignantly to the prancing animal who now had a pinecone in her mouth. A leaf clung to the dog's backside.

"It's Christmas time. Everything gets a little magical touch." Cecelia rubbed her fingers together, pantomiming the sprinkling of pixie dust. She then did the motion over Oscar's head. "Even you, Mr. Grumpsters."

Oscar's eyes opened wide behind his thick glasses. "What the? I'm not—" he sputtered.

"You are. You are. You are," interrupted Cecelia, her voice all lightness and sweet, like how he'd imagine Mrs. Claus. "Grumpy as the day is long."

Oscar harrumphed loudly, a gift he'd perfected through much practice during his eighty some odd years.

"Oh, come on, smile. Everyone loves a happy face." Cecelia tapped the dimples in her pink cheeks, miming what she was encouraging him to do.

Oscars scowl deepened. He did not smile on command.

She danced the last few steps over to him and tucked her soft fingertips into the corners of his lips. Ever so slightly she pushed up. As soon as she released, his mouth dropped again.

She frowned. "Oh, dear. Those muscles haven't been used very much at all. You have a bit of atrophy going on there. Give it a try. You can do it."

He blinked, more stoic than ever.

"Oh, pooh." She stepped away, waving the towel at him dismissively, and then glanced up into the sky. "Is that a snowflake? Look, Oscar! It's snowing. Right on time for Christmas! How magical!" Her breath frosted from her mouth in a soft curl. Oscar wouldn't have been surprised if it formed a heart-shaped smoke ring.

He resolutely shook his head. "We aren't going to have any snow this year, I tell you." He said it as if his very words would cause the storm to squeal like a frightened pig and run in the opposite direction.

"Really? Well, let's make a bet, then. How about if it snows you make dinner? If not, I will. I choose lasagna." Without waiting for an answer, she called for the little dog, "Come on, Peanut!"

The dog immediately dropped the pinecone and pranced along the path and up the stairs. She ran two tight circles around Cecelia and then scampered into Oscar's house.

Oscar's lip quivered with indignation. He rubbed his arms and tried to hide a shiver from the chilly air.

"Come on, let's get these groceries unpacked and then

help me get the decorations on the tree." Cecelia tucked her arm into his and bent to help him gather the few bags he'd dropped in the entry way.

Did she say tree? Oscar puzzled over that while they carried the groceries into the kitchen. Cecelia dropped them on the counter and immediately dug into them, smiling as she pulled out her ginger.

Oscar attempted to pull the leaf off the dog cavorting his feet. "Bear! Stand still, will you? What do you have? Ants in your pants?" He plucked the leaf off and continued in the same grumpy tone, "What were you saying about a tree, Cecelia? What tree? I haven't had one of those since the year of the freezing rain."

"Frank brought it over while you were out," she answered, tucking the groceries away. Frank was her grandson, a retired military vet and a current police officer with the Gainesville police force. After shutting the last cupboard, she headed into the living room without waiting to see if Oscar would follow.

Grumbling, Oscar sank into the saddleback kitchen chair to untie his shoes. It hurt his hands, but he soon had them off. As he trailed down the hallway to the living room after her, his nostrils widened as he caught scent of her lingering rosewater perfume hanging in the air. A ghost of a smile flitted across his lips, although he'd never let her catch him doing that.

"Look. Isn't it lovely?" Cecelia exclaimed when he came

around the corner. She waved a hand at the giant tree that sat in the corner.

Oscar's mouth dropped. As far as trees go, it was a rather prestigious display. Fluffy-boughed and spilling the aroma of snappy fresh pine, it stood rather proudly in the corner.

But a tree! In his own house! He pushed his glasses farther up his nose as he stared in horror. And was it… flocked white? It was!

Oscar sank down into his easy chair which squeaked and squished from the years of accommodating him. He dug his toes into the worn flannels slippers he kept tucked under the coffee table. Bear jumped up and snuggled into his lap. Not that he'd say she was snuggling—more like hogging all the space. He dropped his hand to stroke her soft ears, and she gave his hand a little licky-kiss.

The pup's warmth calmed him, and he finally found the words to make an indignant objection. "What is the meaning of this? You can't just put up a tree in someone's home! They're dirty, and lose needles, and have spiders."

"Oh, poo! Are you telling me that you're afraid of a little spider?" Cecelia lifted the dog off his lap and held out a hand to help Oscar up. "Come on! It's time to make new memories."

He stared at the tree grudgingly but slowly stood. He would never breath a hint of it, but sometimes he was no match for her. She kissed his cheek, and he smiled. Then she set down Bear and handed him a box of ornaments.

Oscar glanced at the menagerie of ornaments in his

hands, everything from gingerbread houses, to ice-cream cones and rocking horses. "How are ice-cream cones about Christmas?"

She was already at the tree placing candy canes.

Before she could answer, a fierce knocking rattled the front door. Bear exploded into barking and raced down the hall with a furry kick and a puff of fur.

Who could that be? Oscar wondered, stomping after her. He reached the door with Bear running in circles around his feet.

"Watch it, ya billy-pup. You're going to trip me."

The dog ignored him. She continued to jump, with every third leap bringing her eye level to a skinny window next to the door. That was her power move, and she added an extra-intense note to her bark to show it.

Oscar wrenched the door open.

On the other side was a short man. He glanced dully at Oscar while weakly grasping the door frame. The man wore jeans and a thin jacket despite the cold temperature. His feet sported gray sneakers. As Oscar watched, the man slowly slumped to his knees. The stranger gasped, "Water." Then he collapsed onto the worn straw welcome mat, one hand landing on Oscar's freshly-slippered foot.

CHAPTER 2

Footsteps pattered rather frantically down the hallway, and a breathless Cecelia patted his back. "Oscar," she puffed. "What is it? What's going on?"

"Stay back," he warned. Knees creaking, he lowered himself down to nudge the man on the shoulder. "Buddy, what's the matter with you? You okay?"

"Oscar?" Cecelia's voice wavered. "Oh, my stars! What's going on? Is he hurt?"

Feeling his joints screaming, Oscar leaned down even deeper to feel the man's neck. Seconds ticked by. Sighing, he slowly stood and glanced at Cecelia. "Call 911."

She peered down at the sprawled figure. "Lord have mercy. Oscar! I know who that is! He's a guest at my bed-and-breakfast!"

"You know him?"

Her voice wavered. "Yes, yes. I know him. That there is Mike McElroy. Both he and his father have been with me for two days now. They were supposed to leave tomorrow."

Oscar shook his head. "Well, he's not going home now. Or, you might say he's already arrived."

"He's dead?"

"Deader than a doornail."

Cecelia stuffed her knuckle into her mouth. "Oh, my word. The poor man! What am I going to tell his father?"

"Let's get the phone. This a job for the police to handle."

THE ANCIENT CLOCK on the wall ticked, its glass face cracked from the time one of Oscar's teenaged sons accidentally hit it with a tennis racket. He thought about his sons now—over twenty years had passed since he'd last seen them. What were they doing? Would they ever forgive him?

His face flushed. He couldn't think about that now. He sucked back the emotions and glanced across the kitchen table at Cecelia. "How you doing?"

"Well, to be honest, I feel like I can't breathe until the emergency personnel get here. I even thought about opening the kitchen window. I swear it's like some strange sort of claustrophobia."

Oscar nodded. "It is pretty odd. And here we are, staring at each other like two store mannequins."

"I don't even know how to act." She sighed and stirred

her tea, cold and ignored except to be used to spin her spoon again and again. "This is all so sad. It's bringing to mind how important it is to make an effort to not fight with your loved ones. Poor Steve—that's Mike's father. The two of them fought like cats and dogs from the moment they checked in to my place. Even something as simple as beverages caused them problems. For example, at breakfast this morning Steve asked his son if he wanted some coffee, and Mike answered that he hated coffee and only drank energy drinks and to leave him alone." She shook her head. "Those drinks are such a nasty habit. I bet they contributed to Mike's bad attitude."

Then Cecelia flushed with self-reproach, realizing that the man she'd just said had a bad attitude was lying on the front stoop.

After that, the conversation between Oscar and Cecelia petered out with the silence only being broken by the clock and the tapping of Cecelia's spoon.

Finally, the sounds of sirens came down the street, making the couple sigh in relief. Yet the two were soon flung from one bizarre set of circumstances and into another as the surreal calm they'd been trying to swaddle themselves with was shredded with emergency personnel scuttling about the porch and through kitchen.

It was a rather nice surprise to Cecelia to see that one of the officers was her grandson's police partner.

"Evening, Ms. Wagner," said the young officer, nodding his head. His name was Jefferson, and his body was shaped like a Slim Jim jerky stick. His clean-shaven face was serious now. Come to think of it, no-one had ever saw him smile much.

Officer Jefferson asked, "So you're saying this man was a guest at your bed-and-breakfast?" He jerked his thumb in the direction of the thick hedges that divided Cecelia's place from Oscar's home.

Cecelia patted her bun, searching for stray hairs, as she nodded. "Yes, both he and his father. Oh, my stars. His father doesn't even know what just happened. One of you all need to go tell him." She stood on her tip-toes to see out the window. "I'm surprised there are no guests wandering about outside right now, wondering what the commotion is over here."

"It's actually not so surprising. On cold days people tend to stay inside. Now, exactly how would you describe the father and son's relationship?"

Cecelia shrugged and glanced at Oscar who had appeared behind her. Peanut was in his hands and he absentmindedly stroked her. The dog had settled down like she knew being in his arms was her place of safety.

"Go on and tell them," he encouraged, knowing how she didn't want to badmouth the deceased man again.

Her gaze flicked up at the officer. "Would you like a cup of tea?"

"No tea for me," Officer Jefferson said.

Cecelia dumped her cold tea, slowly refilled it with water, and then stuck it in the microwave. She thought she was being subtle, but it was obvious she was taking a moment to regroup her thoughts and consider how she would answer the officer.

Finally, she began. "Well, I'd say they were a bit combative, the two of them. Fathers and sons often are." She winced slightly after saying that, knowing how Oscar had no contact with his own boys.

Oscar gave no reaction as he gently set the dog back on the ground. Peanut immediately scurried over to sniff Officer Jefferson's shoes.

"What types of things did they fight about?" Officer Jefferson asked. He had his pad out and was taking notes.

"Steve—that's the father—Steve is recovering from a car accident he was in about six months ago. It was horrific, and he is now in a wheelchair. They had just settled with the insurance company and were out here as their first trip away from all the hospitals and stress." She shook her head. "Those poor men. I think the stress was getting to them, and that's why Mike was feeling impatient with his father."

"Hey, can I help?" A familiar face poked his head into the kitchen. It was Frank, Cecelia's grandson.

At the sight of Frank's concerned face, Cecelia breathed in relief. "Oh, Frank, it was Mike. Did you see him? I'm not sure what happened. Could it have been a heart attack? He always drank those energy drinks. He was so young."

Frank glanced at Jefferson and then back at his grandma. His lips pressed together. "From what I'm hearing there's a strong suspicion he was poisoned."

Shocked, Cecelia reeled back into Oscar, who caught her

elbow. Peanut caught the excitement and pranced about barking. There were several chaotic moments with Oscar yelling, "Bear," while the dog raced between everyone's legs.

Finally Frank caught her. He locked her wiggling body down with his elbow, quickly averting his chin as she tried to give him kisses. "Unfortunately, the police need to go over to your place, Grandma. They need some samples of the food to rule out where Mike might have come into contact with it. In fact, if you could make a list of everything you saw him eat, the coroner would really appreciate it."

Cecelia's mouth puckered as though she might cry. "What are you saying? Are you saying it's my cooking? I can't see what he would've eaten that was bad. Everyone had the same oatcakes, and fruit. I saw him eat a doughnut, and he did ask for a cup of Greek yogurt. You know how he was about protein. And those darn energy drinks. I never saw him without one."

The paramedics had finished loading up the body, and the ambulance headed back onto the road.

Frank nodded, scratching the dog's ears. "All right, well, we're heading over to give the news to his father. Maybe you should wait a few minutes before you join us. Don't feel obligated if you don't want to come right away. I can show the detectives around the kitchen."

He set the dog down and left with the rest of the policemen.

Oscar and Cecelia looked at each other as silence descended again.

"You okay?" Oscar asked.

Cecelia puffed out her chest and crossed her arms. "How can my own grandson think I'd be okay waiting here? With strangers poking around my kitchen? I hardly think so. Besides, I have a responsibility to the other guests. Steve is kind of fragile. I don't know what he is going to do. Poor guy, he's all alone now."

Oscar raised an eyebrow. "How comfortable is he with the wheelchair?"

"Not very, even with Mike's help. That was a big part of their fight. Last night Mike threatened to put his father in a nursing home if he didn't get his act together."

"Did anyone else hear him say that?" Oscar asked.

"Oh, for sure. The whole argument was very uncomfortable. We were all playing rummy—well you know. You were there."

Oscar did know. If he recalled correctly, Mike was the reason they'd all played rummy. Steve had wanted to play poker. Mike had been very upset because he'd never played poker before.

Their bickering might have stood out more to Oscar except that his attention had been captured by another one of the guests, a businessman named Roy. When Roy had accepted his cards, his sleeve had raised up, exposing the man's thick wrist. It also showed an interesting tattoo, one of a bull that Oscar had seen many times as an FBI agent. He'd been tempted to ask Roy about it, but then the game swept along at a furious rate, Roy's sleeve slid down, and Oscar realized he was actually quite tired. Oscar had left soon after that, blaming the fact that Peanut was lonely, when really his lumbago was acting up. Not to mention he needed to catch his Wheel of Fortune.

In leaving early it seemed that he'd missed Mike berating his dad. "Tell me more," Oscar said.

"Well, Mike was furious because Steve bumped the table, jogging everyone's drink. Glasses splashed, and more than one was knocked over. Everyone jumped back. It was a sight, I tell you, and that round ended because no one was certain whose cards were whose by the time everything was mopped up. I'll never forget how beet red Mike's face was when he proceeded to scold his father that he was a perfect example of why they put old animals out to pasture. Mike said it was time for Steve to find someone else to help him, because he wanted to go their separate ways."

"What a kid," Oscar said disapprovingly.

"It was horrid. Steve said they were stuck together, and Mike said he'd find a way to get away." Cecelia shook her head. "I know that poor young man just died, but last night I can tell you that everyone at that table gasped."

"I would have come unglued."

Cecelia nodded. There was no doubt Oscar would have put Mike in his place. "We were all so shocked that he would be so rude and disrespectful to his dad. After that, Mike stormed out of the house, leaving all of us to try to pick up the pieces. Honestly, the night was ruined with everyone heading to their rooms." Cecelia sighed. "Before I finished cleaning the kitchen, I did take a minute to speak to Steve myself. 'Does he always talk to you like this?' I asked him. 'Because that's not okay.' Steve told me no, in that adamant way of his, and slowly pushed his wheelchair back into their room. I'm not sure when Mike returned."

Just then, through the window Cecelia saw Frank heading back their way.

CHAPTER 3

Cecelia walked out onto the porch to meet him. The crisp air smelled of pine and frost with just a hint of smoke from a neighbor burning a pile of leaves.

Frank walked with lowered eyebrows and matching frowning lips.

"What's the matter?" she asked, crossing her arms against the chill.

He crunched over the gravel driveway. "It's kind of a mess over there. We discovered Steve sleeping in his wheelchair. Apparently, he was waiting for Mike to return from his walk, and they had plans to visit the local pub this afternoon. It was a horrible shock to the poor guy. I asked for Doctor Reynolds to come by and take a look at him."

"Oh, the poor dear." Cecelia clucked her tongue and shook her head.

Before she could ask more, Frank continued, "Grandma, I do have some more bad news."

"More bad news?"

Her grandson stared at the ground, his hand rubbing the back of his neck like he was kneading dough. Finally—with a look of ripping off a bandaid—he raised his head and blurted, "There's talk that they might try to pull your license to serve food until we figure out what killed Mike."

"Talk? Who's talking?"

"One of the other cops. He's new, a transfer from Pittsburgh. I swear he's chomping at the bit to make a name for himself and show us "small town cops" how big city folks do it." Frank rolled his eyes. "I don't think it will come to anything, but I still want you to be prepared."

"Oh, Oscar, what will I do if that happens? What kind of bed-and-breakfast doesn't serve breakfast?"

"We'll figure it out." Oscar patted her back to reassure her. Inside, he was uneasy. He knew how those little wahoos could get when they wanted to make a reputation for themselves in a new precinct.

"As for your other guests," Frank continued, "So far no one has checked out. Sarah told us that she has plans to visit the Amish village later today. Roy and Troy were intercepted as they were heading out for their business meeting, and said they last saw Mike at breakfast. As you can imagine, everyone is quite shocked."

"And there is a doctor with Steve?" she asked.

"Along with Sarah. When I left, she was getting him some tea."

Well, that did it. It was easy to see from the expression on Cecelia's face that she wasn't about to tolerate another woman squirreling around in her kitchen. "I'm heading over," Cecelia said, arms crossed. She marched down the stairs and crossed the lawn, her steps firm.

While she walked, she thought about the guests. Sarah was a nice girl and would be very helpful in comforting Steve. Roy and Troy had kept to themselves the entire time that they had been at the house. However, Cecelia knew that they weren't too happy with Mike's treatment of Steve. Last night, she'd overheard them outside when Roy had been smoking a cigarette. He'd muttered how "Mike's a punk kid," and "when I was growing up, you never treated your elders that way."

Troy had agreed and said that someone needed to teach that kid some manners.

Cecelia rubbed her brow as she walked. Was there something else he'd said? Something about insurance? She'd been so upset about Mike and Steve's fight that she hadn't paid enough attention.

Oh well, she supposed it didn't matter, now. It wasn't likely that they'd be suspects anyhow.

Coincidentally, she was met by one of the businessmen, Troy, who stood on the front porch smoking. His face was glum, and he gripped his cigarette between nicotine-stained fingers.

"I supposed you've heard, eh?" He squinted at her as smoke clouded around his head like a demented halo.

Well, she was hardly going to tell him that it had been both Oscar and her who'd discovered the body. She responded with a stiff nod.

"Did you see that car?" He stabbed the cigarette in the direction of a blue sedan tucked along the side of the house. She glanced over with a jolt of surprise. She'd actually missed it.

"Your new guests are here. Some guy and his gal. They've been wandering around this place for hours," Troy took another drag before stubbing the butt out next to the rose bush. Cecelia wrinkled her nose. Normally the smoking section was in the back of the building, away from the doors. But, since these weren't normal times, she'd overlook it.

"Thank you, Troy," she answered, continuing up the steps.

"Is there anything you need from me?"

She paused while opening the screen door. The green Christmas wreath, with its clumps of red ornaments and bells, waggled with the movement. That was quite nice of him. Unexpected. "Would you mind emptying the trash and maybe dragging the can to the end of the driveway? Tomorrow is pick up."

"Absolutely. It would be my pleasure. By the way, those ribs you made for lunch were out of this world."

"Aw, I'm glad to hear it. Thank you again, Troy."

As she entered the house the warm scent of cinnamon and fresh-cut pine sap greeted her. Now what should she do first? Talk to the new guests or go comfort Steve? And were those cops still in her kitchen?

A loud clatter came from the kitchen, answering her question. She puffed her cheeks in a frustrated sigh. But she'd hardly headed that way when her attention was grabbed by laughter in the living room.

She peeked inside. The new guests were sitting at the table, playing cards that were laid across the cheery red runner in a suspicious pattern of Hearts.

Cecelia sniffed. Well, they'd certainly made themselves at home, especially if they'd been here for hours. Nothing to do about it now.

She walked into the living room with a smile. "Hello, there. I'm Cecelia, the owner of Baker Street bed-and-breakfast."

The man stood at the sight of her and held out his hand. "Bobby. Sorry, I know we arrived early. We'd been hiking all morning, so it was nice to sit down in this wonderful place. And then we saw the cookies and doughnuts, and, well, they called our name."

"It's perfectly fine. That's what the pastries are there for." Cecelia shook the woman's hand as well. "We do have a bit of an emergency that we are in the midst of right now."

Bobby's face fell. "I know, we heard. I'm so sorry."

Silence descended in the room, rivaling that of a library. The young couple glanced at each other. Cecelia tried to interpret the glance. They must be worried they were going to get *that* room.

She rushed to reassure them. "First of all, the dreadful thing that happened to the poor young man occurred off site. His room is downstairs, and the room you reserved is upstairs. Obviously, things have changed now. Perhaps you don't want to stay anymore? With the circumstances, I'll be happy to reimburse your charges. I leave it up to you."

"Oh, no. We definitely want to stay," Brenda said. She carefully picked up the cards and shimmied them back in the box.

Bobby gave an easy grin. "Yeah, it seems that all the hotels are packed. And the day is getting kind of late now. We felt pretty fortunate to get a place at all."

"Everything usually is booked at this time a year," Cecelia admitted. "It's funny. Since it's Christmas time, you'd think that people wouldn't want to leave their homes. But in reality, it seems many folks want to celebrate where they don't have to do the work. And I love sharing Christmas with others."

She really did. She'd had guests for every Christmas the last few years since she'd had the bed-and-breakfast. Every year she made her special Christmas Star bread, and she had fun placing a small present on everyone's bed each morning of the week leading up to Christmas. The presents were only tokens, such as a bar of scented soap or a sample size lotion. Occasionally, she'd give a tiny package of wildflower honeycomb from the hives down the street.

Plus, she had a chance to decorate. She waved a hand now in the direction of the front window which was festooned with fresh green garland and red ribbons. And then in the general direction of the buffet, where the couple had already discovered a silver pump pot of hot cocoa, a jar of marshmallows, homemade doughnuts, Christmas cookies, and a box of sweet peppermint candies. "As you can see, I quite enjoy celebrating it. I'm pleased you will be staying, and hope to make your holiday special."

"I think it will be. We really didn't want the headache of setting up a tree. After all, it's only the two of us, so can you blame us? Look at how cozy this is." He smiled appreciatively at the Christmas tree with its soft white lights and the row of stockings over the fireplace.

More clinking and clanking came from the kitchen. Cecelia cringed, but forged on. "There are a few guests who are checked in, and you might meet them tonight. There's a woman staying down the hall and two business men in the room directly across from you."

"Was that one of them outside just a minute ago?" Brenda asked.

"Yes. They've been at meetings every day since they checked in, but in the evening we have a good time. Everyone lodging here is a fun group. Although, I think tonight might be more somber."

A pot falling made its tinny interruption. Cecelia sighed. "Let me go get the final paperwork for you to sign."

"Oh, I thought we filled everything out online," Brenda said.

"I only need a few more things, such as what vehicle

you're driving, verification of your credit card, and a signature on the rental agreement."

"Sounds great." Bobby smiled.

Cecelia left for the study to get the admission form. On her way, a troop of policemen passed her in the hallway, their boots leaving mud clumps that made her frown. Jefferson held a box filled with what she assumed were food samples. He wouldn't look at her, instead turned his face toward the ground as if ashamed.

One of the cops moved in her direction. He was short, and bristly, and someone she didn't recognize. "Ms. Wagner, We've finished for today. Depending on what the coroner says, we'll let you know if you can keep your food service license."

Cecelia opened her mouth to respond, but he stopped her with a stiff hand. Staring her down, he reached into the box and pulled out a jar of her homemade jelly.

Her eyes flew open. That was one of her special jars!

"I noticed no expiration date on this. That's against the health code," he said.

"Well, it's written right there with last year's summer!" Cecelia cried as she pointed.

"That's not a complete expiration date." He dropped the jar back in the box and then helicoptered his hand to direct the other cops to move out.

Cecelia watched them leave the house, shooting negative thoughts at the pompous little man, and then glanced into the living room.

Both Brenda and Bobby hunkered over their phones, looking a whole lot like two people who were pretending they'd heard nothing.

She shook her head. Would that be all it took? A jar of jelly in the fridge without an expressed expiration date? She'd always just marked them with the year of that summer's harvest. Sighing, she hurried into the study and grabbed the application and a pen and headed back.

As she approached the living room again, she heard Brenda say, "Odd that the host said the man on the porch was at meetings all day. You know we saw them hanging outside that one bar."

Cecelia bustled through the doorway. "Let's finish getting you booked in. Here are your keys. Will you be staying in for dinner?"

"That sounds perfect," said Bobby as Brenda perused the paperwork.

Just then, Sarah, the woman from room 202, walked to the living room doorway. She was a young woman, on winter break from college. At the moment, Sarah's forehead wrinkled with a worried expression, and she clung to the door frame. When she saw she'd caught Cecelia's eye, she said in a low voice, "I'm so sorry to disturb you. Do you have a minute?"

"Of course." Cecelia continued to the new guests, "I'll leave you two to read over the contract, and I'll be right back."

At the doorway, Sarah gently drew her around the

corner. Cecelia wanted to thank her for helping with Steve, but before she could begin, the young woman whispered, "I don't want to alarm you, but I heard those guests say something strange before you came in."

Strange was not a word Cecelia wanted to hear right now, especially in light of poor Mike. She glanced toward the living room before whispering back, "What did they say?"

"They said they got here too late." Sarah bit her thumb nail.

"Oh, that could be in reference to so many things," Cecelia waved her hand dismissively.

Sarah shook her head, adamant, and whispered, "They said they were too late, and the boss wasn't going to be happy with what had happened."

Cecelia frowned. This might be something Frank would be interested to know. "Alright, hon. I'll pass it on." And then with a smile, "Thank you for taking care of Steve. How are you doing? Can I get you anything?"

"No, I'm good. Steve seems to be handling all of this quite well. He asked for some time alone, so I'm going to keep my plans to head out to Sunnyside."

It was a well known Amish restaurant. "You'll love it there. Make sure you get a bowl of their apple crisp!"

At that moment, there was a knock on the front door. The door opened, and Oscar walked through. "Everything's settled at my house, so I came over to see how it's going."

Sarah scooted past him with a wave goodbye.

Cecelia fanned her face as she answered, "The police just

left, and I have two new guests signing in. It just doesn't end around here."

"Have you had a chance to check on Steve yet?"

She shook her head. "You think I should? Sarah said he wanted some quiet time."

He rubbed his bristly chin and nodded. "Maybe a quick check in. You mind if I go with you?"

She nodded. After confirming that Brenda was still filling out forms, Cecelia beckoned Oscar to follow her. they walked down the hall to where there was a bedroom at the end, the only one she rented on the bottom floor.

Cecelia let Oscar set the pace. She knew how his joints bothered him, and with the temperature drop, it was a bear for him. In truth, she needed a moment to regroup her thoughts herself.

Once outside the door, Cecelia glanced at Oscar for reassurance. He nodded his head with a grim smile. She lightly tapped on the door while Oscar adjusted a picture frame sitting on the hall's bookshelf. Cecelia saw him frown when he spotted a pen poking out behind the frame.

"Interesting," he mumbled.

From inside the room there came a feeble, "Come in."

She shot Oscar an anxious look, eyebrows puckered together, and then twisted the doorknob. "Steve? Hello. It's Cecelia and Oscar."

Steve lay in bed, the covers pulled up his chest. He opened red-rimmed eyes.

"Oh, Steve, I'm so terribly sorry." Cecelia rushed to the side of the bed, while Oscar remained inside the door.

Steve mumbled a stream of unintelligible grief-filled words. Cecelia sympathetically patted his arm and murmured words of comfort. She searched for tissues and handed him a few. Finally, he calmed to the point where his words made sense.

"I'm not sure how long I can stay here. I've contacted a temp agency to hire someone to come help me," Steve stammered.

"Shh, you stay as long as you'd like." Cecelia straightened his sheet. "I'm going to go make you some soup. Do you need any help now?" She glanced toward the attached bathroom. "I'll get Frank in here."

"No, thank you. I can get in and out of bed, and into the bathroom by myself as long as the wheelchair stays in reach."

"Okay, but you'll call me if you need anything?"

"I promise. Thank you, Cecelia," Steve smiled weakly.

With a final pat on his arm, Cecelia moved the glass of water closer. She found his phone and placed it on the side table, while Oscar stooped with a groan to pick up a dropped prescription bottle. He glanced at it and placed it on the dresser. Together, they headed out.

As they shut the door, Oscar whispered. "Did you notice that?"

"Notice what?"

"His room, the scent in it."

"Scent?"

"Yeah, a very strong scent of aftershave."

She paused, her thin eyebrows raising. "No, I don't think I did. I was much too worried about how he was doing. The poor thing. I'm going to make him that soup. And maybe some chamomile tea. That helps with everything."

The front door opened then and the two business men came in, talking in low whispers.

"Wonder what they're saying?" Oscar muttered to her.

"The only thing on my mind right at this moment is the condition of my kitchen." Cecelia walked into the room and spun around, taking inventory.

"How bad is it?" Oscar asked.

"With all the noise I heard, I expected more of a mess. I suspect that Frank and Jefferson made sure they were respectful."

Brenda poked her head into the kitchen. She delivered the forms, and mentioned they were heading upstairs to their room.

Cecelia gave her a wave. "Relax and make yourself at home. Dinner will be at five."

As the guest left, Cecelia glanced at the clock. She jumped. "Oscar, where has the time flown to? I'm late!" She spun around the counter. "Let's see, here. I made some rolls this morning. If you could just bring them out to the table, dear, that would be lovely." She bustled over to start a tea kettle and then pulled out cutlets to prepare dinner.

Oscar meandered over to the bread box and pulled out a basket covered with a red-and-white checkered napkin.

Underneath were layers of fluffy buttermilk biscuits. He carried the basket into the dining room. From here he had a clear view of the crackling fireplace in the living room, part of the couch and one wingback chair.

Roy and Troy were standing to the side of the couch. Roy, the taller one, jabbed his index finger into the other man's chest. "We leave tomorrow. You just need to keep it together until morning."

As if sensing Oscar watching, Roy looked over. He immediately stepped away from Troy and raised his hand in greeting. "Nice to see you, Oscar. Dinner ready?"

Oscar lifted the basket in his hand. "If you hurry. I might demolish them all since I'm pretty hungry tonight."

"Oh, we'll give you a run for your money," said Roy, chuckling. "I just need to get something from the room, but we'll be right there."

Oscar watched them go upstairs with a bemused expression on his face. He remembered the tattoo on Roy's arm. "I've got my eye on you," he muttered under his breath. Then he lifted the napkin to peek at the biscuits. "Cecelia! Where's the honey!"

CHAPTER 4

*D*inner was a quiet affair with somber faces as people tried to process the day's events. Uncertainty was on everyone's face, written in wrinkles on their foreheads or drawn mouths. There was occasional flinching if a fork scraped too loudly against a plate, along with an apologetic look. Most everyone cleaned their plates, eating every bite in an effort to avoid conversation.

Poor Steve was still in his room resting. Cecelia had brought him the promised soup, but the last she'd checked, it had remained untouched.

After the meal was over, the stuffed guests slowly pushed themselves away from a messy table and meandered like bears nearing hibernation into the living room. The food had mellowed the mood, and the fire in the stone fireplace crackled welcomingly.

Oscar noticed that more than one guest gave the card table a sharp look as they sank into the easy chairs and plump couches scattered about the room. He assumed they were all thinking about the fight that had happened there the night before.

Cecelia offered everyone spiked eggnog. After a glass or two, the group seemed to ignore the nervous energy that permeated the house like static electricity, and settled into relaxed conversations filled with small talk.

Oscar had waved off the eggnog and instead nursed a cup of coffee in his favorite easy chair. He'd claimed the chair a while back and somehow every guest that had rotated through the doors seemed to subconsciously know not to use it.

He settled back in the worn cushions now and sighed contentedly. It was an amazing chair, with the cushions already melding into his shape. He leaned over his coffee and blew, causing his shoulders to bow forward like two bird wings, and then took a slurpy sip. After he settled back, he barely moved again and nearly blended into his surroundings. In fact, after a few minutes, no one cast him another look.

The new guests, Brenda and Bobby, sat down at the card table, not realizing how the others were avoiding it.

"Anyone want to play?" Bobby asked the group.

Sarah glanced around the room, before shrugging. "Sure." She sat down across from him, and Brenda slid the deck of cards over for her to shuffle.

The two business men glanced at each other. "Maybe another time," Troy said. He then called out to Cecelia, who was pottering around with a tray of Christmas cookies. "That was a great dinner. And I got the trash can out to the road."

"Thank you for doing that. I'm glad you enjoyed it. Do you both have meetings tomorrow?"

"Not sure. Maybe one more day. I'll know more in the morning."

"Well it would be nice if you can squeeze some sight-seeing in to your trip," Cecelia added before carrying the plates into the kitchen.

Roy stood up and stretched. "Good advice. In fact, we're going to head out right now for a bit. Find out if this town has any nightlife." He glanced at Troy. "You ready?"

"Have fun," Sarah said, making the cards bridge in her hands.

Oscar observed the men leave, wondering where they really planned to go.

"So, how are you doing?" Brenda asked Sarah, her voice low and full of sympathy.

"I just can't believe he's gone," Sarah said shuffling through the cards.

"This really affected you, then."

Sarah's cheeks filled with a hot flush. "Yeah, he was a nice guy."

Brenda said nothing, but watched Sarah.

Sarah caught the look and sighed. "This is silly, but I

thought he might be interested in me. I was sort of expecting him to ask me out."

"Aww," Brenda tipped her head sympathetically.

"Although, I never would have said yes." Sarah paused, her eyes introspective as she shuffled again and again. She murmured. "Because he wasn't always so nice to his father. I wonder how's Steve doing, anyway?" Her gaze swept down the hall toward the bedroom.

Cecelia came in with a plate of cookies. "I caught the last thing you said. The poor man's asleep now."

"I wonder how he's going to deal with all of this? Will they be sending Mike's body someplace to bury?" asked Brenda.

Cecelia shook her head, wondering how Brenda knew his name. Did someone tell her? "I have no idea. I just hope there's someone on the other end to help him."

"You think he needs help to take care of himself?" Brenda raised her brows.

"He's still learning to work his wheelchair," answered Cecelia.

Sarah passed out the cards. "Didn't they just win a huge insurance settlement? I think they have money. He can afford to hire someone to help him. And I bet this new person will be nicer than Mike."

Cecelia added more wood to the fire and then settled into her wingback chair opposite Oscar. "The poor man. My mother always said you should never have to bury your children. I'm surprised he's holding up as well as he is."

"Do you know how they got their money?" Brenda asked.

"Shh," Cecelia held a finger up to her lips and glanced anxiously down the hallway.

"Sorry. Earlier today, I heard Troy talking about it. I mean overheard." Brenda shot a guilty look at Bobby.

"And where did you hear them?" Bobby asked, frowning.

"They were in their room."

"You eavesdropped outside their room?" Bobby rolled his eyes and distanced himself from her slightly in the chair.

Sarah chimed in. "She probably couldn't help it. They're so loud, I've heard stuff myself. Honestly, I don't trust those two guys. That isn't the first weird thing I've heard them say." She placed a card on the pile and then leaned forward to whisper to the group. "You don't suppose they are grifters? We don't really know what business they're doing. They leave all day for meetings but where are they really going? Gainesville isn't exactly a metropolis."

Oscar glanced up from his crossword puzzle.

"Well, we saw them outside the bar today when we arrived into town. I recognized them later at the house. From what I saw, they seemed to be having a good time," Brenda said.

Oscar noted that Bobby tapped Brenda's foot under the table. Brenda blushed and stared down at her cards.

"Last night was awful. I wonder how Steve feels about the horrid fight now?" Cecelia added.

"That was one of the most awkward experiences I'd ever

had." Sarah agreed. "And then the pacing in the room, back and forth pacing with those loud shoes."

"You could hear them from upstairs?" Cecelia asked, surprised.

"Yeah, sorry. It came up through the heat vent. I swear it sounded like Mike was roller skating, he was stomping so much. And they were fighting. I couldn't hear what they were saying but their tones were sharp and mean."

"Stomping like he was wearing hard-soled shoes?" Oscar asked.

"Yes, exactly like that. Business shoes. Did you hear it?"

Cecelia shook her head. "I didn't hear anything."

"Well, it was probably nothing, but I swear I heard Mike call his dad by his first name, among other nasty things. He was so mad."

"That sounds terrible," said Brenda, laying out her cards. She won that hand, and the other players groaned.

"Ready for another game?" Sarah gathered the cards.

"Not me. I've got an early morning tomorrow," Bobby said. "You coming, Brenda?"

She glanced at him wide-eyed. Oscar thought he detected a note of surprise. Still, she quickly recovered, "Yes, definitely been a long day."

Sarah glanced at her watch. "You're right, I should actually be getting to bed myself."

For all of the guests' declarations that they were tired, it was with a rather weird uneasiness that everyone slowly rose from the table. Handshakes were exchanged, along with good nights. Slowly the living room emptied.

Finally, Cecelia and Oscar were alone. She began gathering the glasses. "Well, what do you think of that?"

"Interesting. Very interesting."

She shot him a sharp look. "What exactly does that mean?"

"Right now, I have lots of questions with very few answers." He eased himself up, groaning. After stacking several plates, Oscar followed Cecelia into the kitchen. She filled up the sink while he reached into a drawer and grabbed a dish towel to help dry the plates. They moved like a well-oiled machine. Afterward, Cecelia set about to making dough for the morning.

"You're still being very quiet," Cecelia noted.

Oscar gave her a kiss before grabbing his hat. "The brain is sometimes a slow machine."

"I swear I have no idea what goes on in that old FBI head of yours. Well, goodnight Mr. O'Neil. And by the way," she pointed to the windowsill, now heavily lined with several inches of snow. "I like my lasagna with gruyère and ricotta."

He stared out the window before yanking his hat firmly over his balding dome. At the door he turned back. "It will be the cheesiest lasagna you've ever had, madam."

"I'm a sucker for cheesy." She grinned.

He couldn't think of a sufficiently smart comeback and instead hurried out the door to shake his fist at the still falling snow.

CHAPTER 5

*O*scar stomped back through the snow to his house as a spring of anxiety twisted in his gut regarding Peanut. She'd only been alone for a couple of hours. Still, it had been a rough day, and the dog might have picked up on the stress. He climbed up the porch steps and tried to quickly unlock the door, his fingers feeling stiff and cold.

The door swung open, revealing a dark interior. He'd forgotten to leave the light on. There was also no welcoming patter of nails racing along the hardwood. No happy bark.

Oscar hurried into the house, slamming the door behind him. He called out, "Bear!" Concern filled him when she didn't answer, more than he'd ever admit, and he at last resorted to calling her Peanut.

Still no answer.

Feeling slightly breathless he flipped on the kitchen light, and after a quick peek around, stumbled down the hall and into his bedroom. There he found her fast asleep on the bed, curled in a fat comma right in the center of his pillow.

"Dag-nabbit dog, you scared me," he whispered, easing himself down next to her. He stroked her head which awakened her. Then he had to endure a few minutes of doggy kisses.

"Come on, Bear. Let's go for our evening digestive walk." With the snow, he didn't want to chance losing her, so he buckled a leash to her collar— one that still jingled, he noted grumpily.

This was the time of the day he always enjoyed the most, with the shush and darkness wrapping like a flannel robe around him. He enjoyed standing outside, his neck and back creaking with effort as he stared up at the stars. It was a quiet moment to mentally digest all the events that had happened that day. And he had some stuff that needed digesting.

He wandered into his back yard with Peanut tugging on the leash. The dog loved the snow and snuffled through it.

"What are you sniffing at, Bear? Isn't that cold?" he asked, tucking his other hand into his pocket.

The dog looked at him with a huge scoop of snow resting on the end of her black nose. Her tongue lapped out, almost like she was laughing, before hurrying to root through the snow again.

She was a good dog though and seemed to know not to tug on her leash too firmly and jar her owner. She was content to stay near his feet.

Oscar gazed up at the sky. The snowfall had finally stopped. Maybe his angry fist shake had made a difference after all. The clouds were parting now and stars could be seen, extra bright and sharp diamonds in the cold air.

He glanced over at Cecelia's and noticed that Troy's and Roy's room had the light on and the window cracked open. Had the businessmen already returned? Awfully early for a night on the town. Curious, he cut through the hedge and wandered around the side to the back of Cecelia's house. Peanut followed happily, sniffing this way and that.

Oscar stopped under a giant maple tree that grew next to the house. Directly above him was Roy and Troy's window. There was a nice solid bench there which he sank down to gratefully. It was a good spot to rest and reflect. It was also a good spot to eavesdrop.

Above him, the two men were in an argument.

"How long are we stuck here then?" said one that sounded like Troy.

"Until the boss tells us we're done."

"So, what do we do now?"

"What do we do? We don't talk outside this room, that's what we do."

"No one can hear us. They're in the kitchen."

"You need to be more careful. I don't trust that old man. He's too snoopy."

"Please, that guy was a blue-collared worker his whole life. Just look at him. He's beat down, you can see it in his eyes."

Oscar stiffened. As if sensing her owner's indignation, Peanut let out a low growl. He reached down to shush the dog.

Above him came the sound of the window slamming closed. He waited a moment, not certain if they'd seen him, before quietly creeping away.

CHAPTER 6

The next morning Oscar fed Peanut her breakfast and then let the dog out for her morning walk. He eased himself into the porch rocking chair to watch her and was surprised by an unexpected scent of cinnamon. What in the Sam Hill? His gaze bounced down to the decking where a basket filled with giant scented pine-cones sat on the other side of the door frame. Another gift from Cecelia, he supposed.

He gently rocked the chair and watched the dog meander through the melting snow, her nose down. A part of him wondered if he would see Roy or Troy later that day. Would they mention the possibility of spotting him the night before?

He doubted it. They were the type of men who tried to keep things close at hand.

Peanut wandered toward the bushes, still capped with wet snow, that grew near the front of the property. Her nose dug trenches in the snow as she sniffed. She buried her face in deep between the branches and her spine stiffened. A moment later, she disappeared into the foliage.

Oscar stood up from his rocking chair. "Bear! You get back here!"

A moment later the dog burst into intense barking. Frantic. Insistent. She worked her way back through the hedge, her ears raised in alarm and she ran towards him, yipping.

"Bear! Dagnabbit, what's wrong with you girl?"

The dog torpedoed toward him in a yellow blur. Her eyes weren't smiling any longer, rather bulging with fear.

"What's the matter with you, girl?" Oscar said softer and with more concern.

He glanced in the direction that she'd come from. Were the bushes moving? Was someone over there?

Oscar hurried inside. He grabbed his hammer, one with a solid oak handle, that he liked to carry with him. It would deliver some knocks, yes it would.

Peanut ran straight through the open bedroom door.

He eyed the room for a moment and then, deciding she was safe, returned to the porch while shutting the door tightly behind him. He'd take care of business, that was for sure. He pushed up his glasses and slowly made his way down the creaking porch steps. Frank and Georgie, who was

Cecelia's tour guide, had fixed them, but the second tread was stubborn and held on to its creak.

"Anyone out here?" he called toward the hedges, gripping the handrail for balance.

There was no answer.

Slowly he traipsed over Peanut's tracks to where she'd been startled. With the hammer end, he poked through the branches, but didn't see anything. He'd have to go over to Cecelia's side in order to see if there were any tracks. It was the kind left by human's that worried him.

Groaning, he eased himself straight and headed back into the house where he found the dog hiding under the bed. He could hear her gnawing on something. There was no way he could get down on his knees. Instead, he opted to sit on the bed, its springs giving out a rusty squeal.

Leaning down, he yelled, "You have had it, little lady. Next time, I'm going to let the squirrel get you. You hear me? Come out of there this minute!"

The dog crawled out. In her mouth was a bone, wrapped in a napkin. He wrestled it from her just as the phone rang.

He scowled at the dog before making his way into the kitchen for the wall phone. His phone was one of those old-fashioned ones with the long cord, and he was rather proud of it.

It was on its sixth ring by the time he reached it.

"Oscar O'Neil," a very indignant Cecelia hollered. "Your dog got into my garbage and dragged it to Tim-Buk-Tu!"

"Cecelia, my love, this little dog couldn't knock over a paper bag, let alone a heavy garbage can."

"Maybe so, but I saw her leaving the scene with evidence in her mouth!"

He glowered at the animal. "Yeah, well she dragged that bit of evidence under the bed. But I swear it must have been that Golden Retriever up the road. I saw it around here last week."

"Sparky? Surely not. He's the sweetest thing," Cecelia protested.

Oscar rolled his eyes, knowing Cecelia's soft spot for the retriever. "Sweetest thing or not, he's the one who was digging out the trash. I guarantee it." He sighed. "But I'll be over in a minute to help clean up."

"Oh, would you? Thank you, darling. I'll save a homemade doughnut just for you."

Oscar could practically hear the smile in her voice as she hung up. Well, now he'd done it. He was about to spend the rest of the morning picking up bits of paper and bone. His back creaked as he reached to hang up the phone, and he winced.

"Bones are already complaining," he muttered before looking at the rubbish he'd rescued from Peanut. "Interesting," he muttered.

Then, giving out another groan that would rival a rusty gate, he pulled a thick phone book from a kitchen drawer. He still used them, despite Georgie telling him it was outdated.

After a few minutes of huffing and squinting to follow a red-knuckled finger trailing down the alphabetical list, he finally found what he was looking for.

Peanut came from the bedroom and sat at his feet, her happy dog face on again. "You, young lady, are a troublemaker," he whispered as he slowly dialed the number.

Peanut gave a yip back and tipped her head. Oscar was surprised to see her collar had slid off during her travels through the hedge, but at least that confounded bell was gone.

A man answered on the other end. Oscar stared out the window as he asked, "Hello, may I speak with the concierge please?"

AFTER A BRIEF CONVERSATION, he got off the phone. He stared down at Peanut. "That was very interesting. Now you be a good girl while I go clean your mess. I'll be back soon."

The dog pranced after him as he pulled down his wool jacket from the hallway hook. He slowly shrugged into it and searched for his gloves. Of course, today of all days he couldn't find them. He bent to scratch Peanut's head whose twinkling eyes assured him she would be back on his bed pillow the moment the front door shut. Then, after carefully locking the door, he walked over to Cecelia's front yard.

He'd only made it halfway there when he could see that she wasn't exaggerating. Chicken bones, paper, and energy drink cans littered the yard. Slowly, he began gathering the garbage into the can. He set the energy drink cans to one side. It had to have been that Golden Retriever. Either that or those bandit raccoons were back.

He had the area cleaned up quicker than he thought. After replacing the trashcan lid—and this time making sure it was snug—he went around the side of the house with the energy drink cans and to search for a hose to use on his hands.

While he was back there, he heard a voice that sounded like it came from the bench in the back yard under the maple tree. He paused to listen. It sounded like a woman, and after a few sentences, Oscar determined she was on the phone.

"Am I out of the job or what?" Her words were whispered.

He froze to listen. Which of the women was it? Sarah, or the new guest, Brenda?

The whispering continued. "Yeah, but the guy's not going to work with us like the kid." There was a pause. "Okay. Got it."

Oscar waiting a few moments before casually peering around the corner. He was disappointed to find no one there. He hurried back to the front of the house.

Both Brenda and Sarah stood together in the driveway.

"Good morning, ladies," he said.

"Where did you pop out of?" Sarah asked, surprised, jumping back.

"I just finished dealing with that garbage mess and was looking for a hose to rinse my hands." He held them out.

"You picked all of that up? That's why we're out here." said Sarah.

Oscar glanced at his hands, still unwashed. "Well, it's finished now. And now, I'll be heading inside for my reward, a doughnut."

"That's a great reward! They were amazing," Brenda crowed, rubbing her hands to warm them.

The snow started falling again. "Woohooo!" Sarah spun in a circle. "I love winter!"

Oscar felt quite differently, and his feelings of unease only grew as he thought of what he'd overheard.

CHAPTER 7

Oscar entered Cecelia's house to a barrage of Christmas carols that she had playing in the living room. He was stunned to see the lights on the tree actually blinking in time to the beat of the music.

"How in the...?" He shook his head and gave up understanding, instead headed down the hall and into bathroom. After cleaning his hands, he walked to the kitchen for his promised reward.

The picture frame on the bookshelf was crooked again. He stared at it, and then slowly glanced down the hall with his eyebrows lowered in puzzlement.

After straightening it, he continued into the kitchen where Cecelia was rolling a crust for a giant chicken pot pie. Oscar went behind her and kissed her neck. "You look beautiful, my Cherie."

A throat cleared, and Oscar glanced over at the little breakfast nook. Frank sat there, finishing a plate of eggs.

Oscar stepped back from Cecelia. She smiled at him, her plump cheeks flushed from the heat of the kitchen. "Are you here to claim your prize?"

"I am," he said.

She pointed a floured finger to the end of the counter where a doughnut sat on a plate. He took the plate and carried it over to Frank.

"Any word on Steve?" he asked.

Cecelia shrugged. "He seems to be coping. He's asked to be alone, so, other than the time that Frank helped him dress earlier this morning, no one has gone in there."

"He had a coughing fit while I was in there," Frank tacked on.

Cecelia left the dough to stir the stock pot on the stove.

Oscar watched with interest. A hearty beef stock scent permeated the air, and he licked his lips.

"Not for you. This is some soup for Steve. And speaking of dinner, Don't you think I've forgotten about my lasagna."

Oscar stuck a bite of doughnut in his mouth to avoid answering.

"I should go see if he needs help now before I head out for my day," Frank said and gulped down the rest of his coffee.

"Let me join you," Oscar said as he wiped his mouth.

"Well, wait for me," Cecelia added. "I'll see if I can get him to take some of this broth."

A few minutes later, the three of them hovered outside the door.

Frank knocked on the door, "Steve? Is it okay if we come in?"

A weak, "Come in," answered him.

Frank glanced at the two people crowding behind him, before easing the door open. He took a step inside with Oscar and Cecelia close behind. The mug and spoon rattled on the tray in Cecelia's hands.

"How are you doing, Steve?" she asked. "We wanted to check on you. Look, I brought you some broth. Do you feel up to taking a few sips?"

Steve painfully began to scoot up in the bed, his eyes puffy and red. Oscar wrinkled his nose at the still strong scent of aftershave, while Frank hurried over to help him. Cecelia set the tray on the dresser and went to Steve's other side. Together, they supported him under his arms, while he moaned softly, until he was sitting.

Cecelia fluffed the pillows and tucked the blankets and then brought the breakfast tray over. She plucked out its little wooden legs and set it over his lap.

Steve's glazed eyes locked onto her. "I can't thank you enough," he said humbly.

"Were you able to get any rest?" Cecelia asked. "Has everyone been in here bothering you?"

The bedridden man grimaced. "No one's been in besides Frank this morning. I think on top of everything else, I'm getting sick. My throat has been sore, and I've been sneezing."

Cecelia nudged the mug closer. "Try the soup, Steve. My mother used to call it Italian antibiotics."

The man took the mug in shaking hands while everyone in the room pretended not to notice his frail state.

Oscar's gaze landed on a suitcase sat on the second bed. It was already zipped up. A pair of business shoes sat neatly by the bed. Oscar noted they were quite a bit bigger than his own size.

"How are you doing, young man?" Oscar asked Steve.

"Oh, as well as I could be. If you could just get me…." He pointed a crooked finger to the water on the nightstand. Next to it was a prescription bottle. Oscar grabbed the cup and handed it over, trying to take extra care since it was full. He went back for the bottle.

"No, no, I don't need those. Thank you," Steve said, gently waving them back.

Oscar set the bottle back.

"Do you need us to call a doctor?" Cecelia asked, her eyebrows lifted. While waiting for an answer, she filled his water glass from the carafe sitting on the end table.

"No. I'm sick of doctors. Haven't been to one since my last rehab date. Broke my back in the car accident." He threw the last bit at Oscar. "They can't do nothing. I closed the insurance claim and need to learn how to live life."

"What are your plans now?" Oscar asked. "Did you find someone who can come up here to be with you?"

The rim of Steve's eyes seemed to redden even more. The poor guy's eyes were bloodshot. "I'll be going back home today. My brother will help me out temporarily. I called the certified nursing assistants agency, and they are sending someone here to come take me to the airport. Once I'm home, I'll try to pick up the pieces as best as I can. First, I'll give Mike a proper burial. Then, maybe I'll hire a companion with the insurance money and do some traveling."

"That might be for the best." Cecelia patted his leg. Realizing he couldn't feel it, she jerked her hand away like it was a hot stove. "Meet some new people. Take a break from the memories."

"You were close with your son?" Oscar asked.

Cecelia shot him a sharp look. He winced, realizing he would pay for that question later.

"Very close," Steve whispered.

The room felt prickly with awkwardness. Oscar thought it best to make his escape. "If you need anything, please let me know," he said with a nod to Steve.

As he left, he heard Steve reassuring Frank and Cecelia that he was okay for the time being. The two of them followed Oscar into the hall.

Cecelia arched her eyebrow as Frank finished shutting the door. "Not known for your smoothness, hmm?"

"It was an insensitive question to ask," Oscar conceded.

Frank's eyes darted between the two of them. "If you guys are done, I'm heading out now to meet Georgie. We're supposed to have lunch."

"Well, that will be fun. Tell her hi from me. See you soon," Cecelia said. And then to Oscar, "You leaving now as well? Or staying to help me with lunch?"

Oscar frowned instead of answering.

"What are you making that face for?" Cecelia asked.

"What do you mean my face? This is the only face I have!" Oscar scowled more.

"Pish-posh. You have the cutest face, but you're not making it now. What are you thinking about?"

"Before I tell you, do you mind if I visit the study? I'd like to check something."

"What do you have up your sleeve?"

"I have a gut feeling. I need to check it out."

"You and your gut feelings. I keep telling you to take antacid for that. You do what you need to do. I have to go check on my potpie." With that, she waved him off.

He meandered into the study and shut the door behind him. It was cooler in here and dark. The only light came through the window, dim from the new snow storm. He walked carefully over to the desk and felt around for the desk light. He clicked it on and waited, wondering if anyone would come in. When everything remained silent, he reached for a folder that sat square on the blotter. Breathing heavily, he rummaged through it.

There were several sheaves of papers. He pulled out the rental contracts. His rough fingers flipped through the papers until he found the one he wanted. Quickly, he scanned through the questions. His nostrils flared. He glanced at his watch and considered the time difference. Then he picked up the phone and dialed. He was discreet.

CHAPTER 8

*C*ecelia covered the dinner rolls and put them in the warm pantry to rise. Her potpie was bubbling, its warm chicken scent competing with the sweet fruitiness of two more pies, pecan and apple, that were in the oven. Christmas music played and snow softly fell outside. Everything was as it should be.

Except it wasn't. There was something she'd forgotten about… something she was supposed to have told Frank. Like an itch, it kept popping up to bother her. What was it again?

She sighed and untied her apron to hang it up. Hopefully it would come to her later when she saw him again. She finished washing her hands, wondering what Oscar was up to. She thought she heard a bedroom door open and shut. Whose room was that? Steve's? But it couldn't be.

A second later, a man's gruff voice came down the hall. It wouldn't have caught her attention, except it sounded angry.

Her eyebrows lifted. Was that cursing? The words were low and mumbled and decidedly angry. She held her breath, trying to make out what was being said.

"You promised that the money would be there. Why isn't it there?" There was a pause. "Well I don't care about your excuses. Get after them and get it in the account. I don't want to hear any more excuses. What do I pay you for?"

Cecelia tiptoed over to the door eavesdrop better. At that exact moment, the two business men pushed through the door, nearly knocking into her, and walked into the kitchen. Scrambling back, she reached for a dish and a towel. Too late, she realized she was drying a dirty dish.

She was also muddled by the feeling that something wasn't right. The voice she'd heard hadn't sounded like either one of those men. "Hi Troy. Are either of you hungry?"

"No, ma'am. Stuffed," Troy answered. "We ate on the way here."

Cecelia frowned. That didn't make any sense to her. It was Sunday afternoon, and in this old-fashioned town, most of the restaurants that had any food worth eating were packed full. You could hardly find a seat for a corndog around here if you didn't show up early enough. "Was it hard to get a table?"

"We walked right in. Must have been our lucky day." He glanced around the kitchen. "I'd love to have one of those doughnuts I'm smelling though."

More footsteps rattled against the hardwood floors.

It was Oscar.

Cecelia smiled. Somehow, seeing Oscar always made everything feel alright. "Long time no see, handsome. Did you find everything you were looking for?"

"Indeed I have. And then some. Could I ask you to please call Frank to return, please?" He smiled, but the sentiment didn't reach his eyes.

Cecelia's mouth dropped open. Something about his tone unnerved her.

"Just see if he can pop back here," Oscar murmured again. Then he walked back into the living room where he helped himself to some coffee from the refreshment station.

A moment later both Troy and Roy, both eating doughnuts, meandered after him. Cecelia went for the phone.

"Gentlemen, what are your plans for today?" Oscar asked as he settled into his favorite armchair. It squeaked in its comforting way.

Roy walked over to the fireplace and nudged one of the nativity figurines on the mantle with a nail-chewed finger. "Not sure. Looks like a bad snowstorm is headed our way," he said. He shoved the rest of the doughnut in his mouth and picked up an angel. He started to toss it in the air when Oscar cleared his throat loudly. Roy glanced over at him before shrugging and putting it back.

Cecelia soon joined the three of them and gave Oscar a discreet nod.

"The news is calling for eight inches. We might be snowed in," responded Troy.

"Highway shuts down with that much snow," Oscar noted.

Just then, Cecelia noticed her nativity was out of order and walked over to straighten it. Then she moved to the buffet to tidy things up.

There was clattering down the stairs, making everyone look up. It was Bobby, wearing a winter jacket and hat. He carried two suitcases and set them on the foyer's floor with a huff.

"Hey, guys!" Bobby said. "Glad to see you all together so we can say goodbye. I guess Brenda and I are on our way."

"Leaving so soon?" Oscar asked curiously.

Cecelia noted that, oddly, he didn't seem surprised.

"Yeah. I guess we decided to try to make it to her parents' house for Christmas after all. Especially with this crazy storm rolling in. Have you all heard about it?"

Before anyone could answer, a sharp squealing made everyone turn their heads.

"So, I suppose I'll be checking out now, myself," Steve said, pushing his wheelchair into the foyer. He pulled the blanket that covered his legs up a little further. "Do you think someone could help me with my bags?"

Oscar slowly stood up—making the chair's spring squeak again—and glanced down the hall toward Steve's room. There was a pair of suitcases sitting outside the door. "Were you able to get everything packed, Steve? Even Mike's stuff?"

Steve cleared his throat. "Yeah, everything is packed. I double checked, but we didn't bring much."

"Well that must have been hard to do. I'm sorry about that, sir," Oscar offered sympathetically.

Steve looked down at the blanket, but not before they caught that he was misty-eyed. "I can't thank everyone enough for what you've done for me. But you know I've been feeling sick. And everything else, I really need to get home. I'm sure I will recover better there. My ride will be here any minute to take me to the airport."

"Of course. Sometimes home is the best place." Oscar nodded his head. "And do you have someone meeting you on the other side?"

Steve nodded. "My brother will be there."

Brenda came down the stairs now with a hat on her head and a small valise in her hand. "Hi, everybody!" She smiled. And then to Bobby, "Did you check us out yet?"

"Listen, do me a favor. Why don't you two hang on for a second. There was something I've been meaning to ask you." Oscar beckoned. "You too, Steve. Humor me, if you would. Join us in the living room. I have something I've been meaning to say." Oscar waved his hand through the living room entryway.

Steve paused, his eyebrows lifting. He glanced at Oscar inquisitively, but he went ahead and pushed into the room. Brenda and Bobby left their suitcases and followed.

"What is this, some kind of family meeting?" Bobby joked

as he spotted Roy and Troy. They lifted a hand in greeting while Bobby took off his hat.

"Did someone say family meeting?" called Sarah from the top of the stairs.

"Ah, Sarah! Just the person I was looking for," Oscar said. "Can you join us for just a moment?" He sank back into his chair and glanced around at the group. "I know there is a storm coming, and I won't keep you long. Cecelia, can we turn the Christmas music down a notch? And do you have any of those wonderful homemade gingersnaps left from last night? Would it be possible to bring out a plate? You know how I love them."

Cecelia obligingly turned down the music, and then disappeared into the kitchen. She soon bustled back with a plate of cookies which she passed around. As she did so, a familiar face poked through the door.

It was Frank.

"Hey, everybody," the policeman said. He made no mention of the canceled lunch date with Georgie.

"Ahh, just the man I wanted to see," said Oscar, with a crunch on his cookie. "Try these! They are wonderful!"

Frank sat down like he'd been expected, after first grabbing a cookie. He crossed his legs. "Mm, delicious. How's everyone today?"

"Fine, fine," Oscar said. "These lovely people are about to check out of the bed-and-breakfast. They are humoring me right now. I did want to clear up a thing or two before we all went our separate ways."

"And what's that?" Bobby asked from over by the Christmas tree. His forehead rumpled in a display of faint annoyance.

"Yes, yes. Let's get right to the point. After all, everyone is busy. You all have lives. No need to beat around the bush." Oscar swiveled in the chair and pointed to Steve. "You, sir, can walk."

CHAPTER 9

The room deadened with silence. It was so quiet, a mouse couldn't have even snuck by without being heard.

No one moved, as if not wanting to be the first to look at Steve.

After a few shocked seconds, Steve gave a blustering laugh. "What are you talking about? I think that's rather unkind—"

"Oscar," Cecelia warned. A flush crept up her cheeks.

"Well, I'd sure like to hear more." Frank leaned forward earnestly, as a relaxed, open expression stretched across his face. He shrugged his shoulder back, causing his jacket to open and the badge in his chest to twinkle under the blinking Christmas lights. Nodding encouragingly, he took another bite of the cookie.

Oscar pulled out a pen from his pocket. He turned it around in his hands as everyone stared. "It started with this. Ordinary little thing, right?"

No one answered. It seemed like a trick question. Oscar continued, "I noticed the pen the day Mike died, when we were about to enter your room to check on you. Funny little thing, it was tucked behind a picture frame."

He studied it for a moment before holding it out to give everyone a closer examination. It was plain looking, a simple ballpoint pen with a silver click top. Everyone leaned back. No one was impressed.

Oscar pressed the top a few times, making the noticeable clicks. His nostrils flared as he exhaled, and he set it on the table.

Frank picked it up, curiously. He turned it over his hands before holding it up to the light and peering down the length. "It's a video camera," he announced.

The news caused a palatable reaction. People gasped, sucked in their breath, and murmured. Oscar held out his hand to ask for silence.

"It is indeed," he said. "Pointed in such a way as to see down the length of the hallway. It would catch anyone approaching the room. Your room." Oscar bobbed his head in Steve's direction.

Everyone turned to look at him, except Frank. He kept his eyes locked onto Oscar like one does on a magician to catch the trick.

Oscar continued, "The first time I saw it, I purposely turned the picture frame so that it would cover the lens. I didn't have time to examine it then, you see. I only suspected. I figured if I could change its position with no recourse, then it was a simple pen. But when I returned, I saw it had been moved back to its prime viewing spot again.

"When I saw that it had been moved, then I knew. Which led me to wonder, why would anyone care to see who was coming down the hall? It wouldn't do any of the other guests any good. No. The only people it would benefit would be Mike and Steve. And with Mike dead, and the pen moved, it had to be Steve."

"This is preposterous," Steve stammered. "You guys can't believe him! I don't care what he says! You all know me. You know I can't walk."

"Indeed," Oscar said, and continued. "However, my second curious thought happened with a prescription bottle. Yours. I noticed it on the floor the day of Mike's death. I thought it was a danger to you on the floor, inaccessible. I specifically put it on top of the dresser to keep it safe. In fact, I positioned it in such a way that it couldn't be knocked down. It was far enough back that if Steve needed it, he would have to ask someone to bring it to him. Yet the very next time I was in the room, the bottle rested on the table beside the bed where Steve was resting. I asked Steve if anyone had been in his room and he himself admitted that no one had entered but Frank."

At this point, Oscar glanced at Frank. "And you didn't move the bottle. Remember you yourself mentioned it was only to help him dress and nothing more."

"Yes, that's right. That's exactly what happened." The police officer nodded.

"My third curiosity came when I noticed a pair of shoes by the bed, hard-soled business shoes. Quite a bit bigger than my own feet. Although, I myself have small feet, so that might not be so unique. However, the shoes were the same size as yours." He stared pointedly at Steve's feet.

"How do you know they weren't Mike's?" Susan asked.

"A very good question. However, Mike was a short man. Maybe my height. And I unfortunately was a witness to his shoe size when he died on my porch. They were my size."

"So what?" Steve blustered. "I wear shoes. Do you have something against that? Just because I can't walk that doesn't make it a crime."

"No, no. Absolutely not. You are allowed to wear shoes, and I assumed you would. But what you are leaving out is that you were walking a lot. In fact, you did so much pacing that it disturbed Sarah upstairs. She heard your steps marching across the floor, clacking loudly. Like business shoes would do, and not like Mike's tennis shoes."

Steve opened his mouth to protest. He caught Oscar's eye and shut it again.

Oscar glanced down as if in humility. Cecelia immediately raised an eyebrow. She knew that Oscar was many things, and many of them wonderful, but being humble was not one of them.

"Of course," Oscar breathed out, "like you might say, this is all circumstantial evidence. But don't worry, it's not all about you, Steve." Oscar smiled in a camaraderie way. He nodded slowly and turned his attention to the other guests. "There are other interesting parts to this story. Very interesting. One of those things was centered around the time you two showed up yesterday." This time Oscar zeroed in on Brenda and Bobby. They both visibly flinched. "Coincidentally enough, from the moment Mike was discovered, you both were here at the house. Too early for check-in, yet you both made yourselves at home. And then there's you two." He swiveled his head quickly and directed the comment to the business men. "Also both here despite a day of scheduled meetings. Odd. So odd."

There was some throat clearing and a few suspicious glances shot at one another, but for the most part, the group kept very quiet. Fear permeated the room with a sour scent.

Except for Steve. He impatiently plucked at the blanket covering his legs. "This is ridiculous. Are you done with this preposterous song-and-dance? I'm sure my car has arrived, and I have a plane to catch."

"Of course. I don't want to keep you. We are all busy people, with places to go and things to do. There is, however, only one more thing." Oscar cleared his throat. "Cecelia, my love, can you get me a glass of water?"

She nodded and hurried out.

"Now, as I was saying, we have these two sets of guests who are here at the exact time as our poor fellow guest is killed. The coroner did confirm that he was murdered, by the way. Poisoned."

Frank nodded.

Cecelia brought the glass, and Oscar took a small sip. He wiped his mouth. "Thank you, my dear. I seemed to have possibly caught a touch of what Steve has. A cold, you said? Scratchy throat?"

Steve glowered at him, instead of answering.

Unperturbed, Oscar continued, "Now where was I? Oh, yes. As I was saying, both Roy and Troy were purportedly here to attend a business conference. Last night I made a few phone calls to the hotels in town. I am friends with a few of the concierges. Strangely enough, no one knew what I was talking about. It appears that those meetings never existed."

Troy and Roy glanced guiltily at each other.

"Of course, this was not of a great surprise since both of you were seen at a bar during the meeting time in question. It was by Miss Brenda, here." Oscar dipped his glass of water in her direction.

Brenda squirmed like a ruffled chicken at the sudden attention. She quickly blurted, "I wasn't ratting you guys out. I made a simple comment to Cecelia. How was I to know?"

Oscar nodded at Brenda. "Of course. An innocent comment. I can see how that could happen. Where did you two say you were going after this?"

They glanced at each other. "Her mother's house," answered Bobby.

"Interesting. And what state is that?" Oscar smiled with an irritatingly patient expression relaxing the wrinkles around his eyes, similar to a parent questioning a three-year-old.

"We, uh…" began Bobby

"Tennessee," Brenda spouted.

"Tennessee, very interesting." Oscar pulled out a paper from the inside pocket of his jacket. Slowly, he unfolded it. "And not the state I was expecting you to say. According to your hotel application, Miss Brenda, you are using a company card?"

Her mouth opened and shut. One of her fingers immediately started to pick her thumb cuticle.

Oscar eyed her through his thick glasses before clearing his throat. He glanced down to read, "The company being BlueMark Liability Insurance, located in Oregon."

She glanced at Bobby and swallowed fast. Bobby rolled his eyes.

"A few minutes ago, I made a quick phone call to the company. The head of operations was happy to reveal that you are both fraud investigators. Highly recommended, in fact. Is that true?"

Brenda's face paled. She glanced at Steve and then back down at her hands. Steve's gaze became more focused and defiant.

Oscar continued, his voice low and mild. "Very

resourceful, I believe your supervisor said. So my assumption is that you will be following Steve wherever he may be going. Obviously as an undercover operation, perhaps. Although it seems I may have blown that."

Neither one of them responded. The air was so thick with tension it felt stagnate.

Oscar peered through the bottom of his glasses as he continued to read. "Now on to Roy and Troy. It seems you are here under an investigative role yourselves. What are the chances? Although you aren't both aren't here in quite the same legal capacity. You are looking into getting repayment?"

"What are you talking about?" Roy sneered.

Oscar sighed slowly, his nostrils flaring. "I'm guessing your boss hooked Steve and Mike up with false identities, along with a false accident report, doctors reports, etcetera. They were supposed to split the money with you. Yet it seems they chose to vanish, instead."

They blinked at him.

Sighing, he continued. "They took off."

"We don't know what you're talking about," said Roy with a shrug.

Oscar pulled out a ratty napkin. Breathing heavily, he leaned forward and flattened it out on the coffee table. On the front, half covered with barbecue sauce, was a very bold red bull moniker.

"Recognize that?" Oscar asked Frank.

Frank leaned to take a look. He flipped it over using the

camera pen. Written on the back was directions to this bed-and-breakfast.

"This morning my dog got loose. Something or someone knocked over a trash can. My bet is on Sparky the golden retriever. At any rate, my dog got into it before I could stop her. I was frustrated, let me tell you. Especially when she ran past me and hid under the bed with her treasure. It seems she found some of your old ribs wrapped in something else. This." He relaxed against the back of the seat. "It's from a known mafia meeting house in Brooklyn. A house that's very well known in producing identity theft documents."

"You can't link that to me," said Roy. "That restaurant is packed every night. Everyone goes there to eat, even the mayor."

"Are you sure there are no links?" Oscar raised an eyebrow, but the man stared him down. Neither one seemed to be willing to back down. Frank got up and walked out of the room.

"Well, this is awkward" continued Oscar. He grinned sheepishly at the rest of the guests. Then he lasered in on Roy again. "When we were playing cards the other day I happened to notice a tattoo on your wrist. You were grabbing the cards and there was a bull as plain as day."

"Anyone can have a bull tattoo," Roy sneered.

"Why don't you show us?" Bobby asked, suddenly sounding quite curious.

Roy looked at him and then at Oscar, before pulling up

his sleeve. The tattoo was exactly the same as what was on the napkin.

"Even if any of that was true, it's no big deal. We didn't do anything," Troy said. "Maybe we were just going to talk to them. Who knows? Mike died before we had a chance. And we had nothing to do with that." He glared at Oscar.

"Oh, I'm not blaming you for Mike's death," Oscar said.

"What's all this about then, anyway?" asked Troy.

"I think you and Roy were here to collect the money that Mike and Steve owed your boss." Oscar then turned toward Brenda and Bobby. "And I think you two were here to investigate Mike and Steve after they apparently bilked your company for an insurance settlement. I'm assuming your company realized something was off with their identities."

And then he swiveled back to Steve. "You were the trickiest. You made me feel sorry for you, have compassion on your situation. You made me feel, and I resent that. You see, it took me some time, but I finally realized that Mike wasn't your son at all."

"How could you say such a terrible thing?" Steve spat out.

"Truth can be a terrible thing, can't it? Well, despite you saying you were so close, you didn't know he didn't play poker or that he didn't drink coffee but only energy drinks. And I noticed that when we went into your room that day, there was a strong scent of aftershave. That might have worked with any other layman, but I've been in FBI for too long for that to work with me. Everyone in the business knows that it's a common trick to make the eyes red and appear teary."

Oscar took another sip of water. Steve didn't say anything, but Oscar saw his hand drop to the chair's wheel. Oscar continued, casually, "Yes, you are the key to all of this. Mike was your partner, and you both assumed new identities, one of them being someone who'd been in a traffic accident. One way or another you were able to procure the settlement. Through the mafia's ties you had the paperwork you needed to show your injury and identify who was at fault. Everything was going as planned until Mike got himself a little too feisty. You guys argued a lot, hmm?"

Steve didn't answer. His grip on the wheel was so tight, his very arm vibrated.

"You both were frustrated. Pacing at night because of being trapped in the wheel chair all day. So you set the camera up so no one would catch you walking around." Oscar rubbed his chin. "So strange how no matter how hard we try to protect ourselves, there is alway a breach in the wall."

It seemed he was thinking about something else. Oscar shook his head. "Forgive me. Age has the baggage of memories. Anyway, back to my story. Despite your attempts to protect your secret, conversations were overheard, and puzzle pieces to the story were scattered."

"This is preposterous. You all have the wrong man," Steve sputtered.

Oscar slammed his hand on the armchair. "So what

ended up being the tipping point, Steve? Did Mike have one argument too many with you?"

Brenda cleared her throat. "Actually, we figured things out a few weeks ago and Mike was cooperating with us to avoid prosecution. He called us here, and we were here to gather our last bit of evidence."

"I see," said Oscar, and then back to Steve, "That makes sense. So, I assume you knew that Mike was thinking of turning over on you. You spiked his energy drink with Digitalis, the prescription in your room, which is used to help with hearth rhythm. It can also cause immediate cardiac arrest if given at a high enough dose when it's not needed."

Steve half-rose out of the chair, his face white with fury. "I don't know what you're talking about. Mike had a heart attack. Like you said, he was known to always chug those energy drinks. How am I to blame for that?"

Oscar raised his hands. "Blame? How are you indeed? Well, the drug will take a couple more weeks to identify, but between the blood vessel petechiae on Mike's face and the reaction to his heart, the coroner has already raised Digitalis as the probable cause of death to over ninety percent. By the way, I saved the empty energy drink cans when I was picking up the garbage. The forensic's lab can test them for the medicine. I'm fairly sure that is why you asked if he wanted coffee yesterday morning, so you could spike his drink."

"You can't prove a thing!" Steve screamed.

"You have the right to remain silent," Frank said,

reappearing in the room. "Anything you say can and will be used against you in the court of law."

Steve stared at him with eyes the size of saucers. He leaped out of the chair and flung it in the officer's direction. Everyone screamed as he darted through the kitchen and out the back door.

CHAPTER 10

*F*ortunately, Steve did not get far. When Frank had left the room the first time, he'd called for backup. The police already gotten into position by the time Frank made his arrest.

There was no reason to detain the other guests. The detectives were already in contact with the BlueMark Liability Insurance. Eventually, all the evidence was gathered, and the police left (with Jefferson quietly reassuring Cecelia that her food service license was safe).

The remaining guests made a quick retreat, with Roy and Troy being the quickest. In fact, they'd abandoned all of their belongings, only to be discovered later in their room. That caused some excitement for a moment. The police energetically poked through everything, but the energy soon turned tepid when all that was unearthed was a generic pile of dress shirts, pants, and underclothing. Cecelia was rather disturbed to learn there were no toothbrushes, however Frank did find a couple of dog-eared copies of Agatha Christie's Poirot mysteries. Cecelia supposed that was a wash.

It was with great relief when the bed-and-breakfast was finally quiet again. A stillness only broken by soft Christmas carols playing in the background.

Cecelia smiled at Oscar and patted the cushion on the love seat next to her. "Come here, my grumpy man."

Oscar rose from his arm chair, and, after making a quick trip to the fireplace to add some wood and to turn up the music, finally came to sit next to her.

"So, no guests tonight?" he asked, and slowly slid his arm around her. They smiled like the old friends that they were.

"Surprisingly, no. The rooms were supposed to be filled for the week. But even sweet Sarah took off, no doubt spooked by the thought of nearly spending her holidays with a group of mafia men, investigators, and a murderer." She sighed. "No Christmas goodies to give. Not to mention, I had that lovely lunch planned."

"Well, I'm feeling a bit peckish." Oscar smiled at her. "Not that I need that excuse to eat. Your pot pie is heaven on earth."

"Oh, really? Even cold?"

"Even anything, as long as I'm with you."

She reached out to stroke his face, now so dear to her. He could act like an old coot, but she knew him for who he really was. Kind. Smart. Considerate.

"You should bring Peanut over here for some lunch as well," she suggested.

He eyed the falling snow. "You don't mind?"

"You two are a package deal. I already know that."

Oscar kissed her cheek, relishing how soft it was and how sweet smelling she was, and then stood up. He tugged on his hat, squared his shoulders, and walked out to brave the snow.

Cecelia squeezed in next to the Christmas tree and watched him from the big living room window. The tinsel tickled her face, and she let out a sad sigh. They'd completely forgotten to finish decorating Oscar's tree in all the ruckus. His first tree in years! She thought about calling him to say she was on her way over when he returned to the porch with Peanut tucked under his arm.

And something else. A brightly wrapped Christmas present.

She grinned as he locked his door, before she darted away to her own room. In a moment, she had her own gift, a much smaller box, which she tucked in behind one of the cushions in the loveseat.

It was a few minutes before Oscar returned. He was letting Peanut do her business before scooping her up and carrying her to the door. Cecelia opened it before he had a chance to knock.

"Do you have a towel? The varmint's feet have collected snowballs," he said. And then for good measure he turned the dog around and pointed at the posterior. "And her butt."

Cecelia laughed. "Bring her in. I'm sure we can get her dry. If not, I'll stick her in the tub.

It took more than a few minutes with the hairdryer on low to melt the snow chunks, but eventually they all fell off. Then she dried the dog, who squirmed happily, and bundled her in a clean towel.

Oscar cradled the dog for two seconds before the wriggling animal made it impossible for him to hold her safely. She wanted to get down to explore every last square inch and right now!

He set her on the floor where she skidded out of the bathroom like she was a race car pumped full of 110-octane leaded fuel. She charged straight down the hall and into the kitchen. From there she ran into the living room, circled the couch two times, before sliding to a stop in front of the Christmas tree. With a happy yip, she looked for her owner, her tongue hanging out in a contented doggy smile.

"Make yourself at home, Peanut!" Cecelia called.

Oscar cleared his throat.

"I mean Bear!" Cecelia amended.

Oscar rolled his eyes and grabbed Cecelia's hand and brought her over to the love seat. Then he retrieved the package he'd left in the foyer, and with a heavy breath of someone who was doing a lot of exercise, set it heavily in her lap.

"Merry Christmas to the cutest cookie-making, sweet-smelling, smart, funny, creative woman I've ever met. God gave me a gift in letting me meet you."

"Oh, Oscar." His compliment took her breath away. Cecelia had met his wife years ago, before she'd passed. She knew what a wonderful woman she was. Tears burned her eyes. "Thank you." And then her eyes sparkled. "But don't think for one moment that I've forgotten about that lasagna you owe me."

He harrumphed. "Just open it."

She did open it to discover a large book. It was of the Caribbean."

"Open it," Oscar coaxed.

She did, and together they studied the beautiful pictures of azure blue ocean scenes, sandy beaches, and lush forest life with waterfalls.

Sitting between the pages about halfway through the book was a stiff white envelope. Glancing at him, a little apprehensively, she pulled it out.

"Go on," Oscar encouraged.

She slid her fingernail under the seal and opened the envelope.

Inside was a piece of paper. She plucked it out and pulled her readers up on the chain and placed them on her nose. It was an itinerary. Her lips moved silently as she read.

"Oh my goodness!" She finally exclaimed. "Is this real?"

"You deserve it," he said. "Two weeks on the Royal

Caribbean. They have a spa on board. I reserved the entire treatment."

Her hand dropped to her lap. "It's too much."

"It's not at all too much. Besides, I'm going as well. In my own cabin," he added, quickly.

She laughed, and he grudgingly said, "Right next to yours. Anyway, you are always doing stuff for others. Always putting people before yourself. I wanted to do something that would let you know that I see you. I hear you, and you are so important to me."

"Oscar…." She didn't say more, instead letting her kiss do the talking. It was quite a few minutes before she broke apart from him with a start. "Oh, my goodness, I have something for you as well!"

She dug behind the cushion and pulled out the tiny box. But as she held it, Oscar noticed her hands were trembling.

"You okay?" he asked.

"Yes." She bit her bottom lip and looked decidedly Not Okay. He reached for the box, and she would not let go. Chuckling, he gave it a little tug.

She hung onto it like a mouse with a piece of cheese.

"You want to give this to me or not?"

Her eyes were wide and maybe a little scared as she looked at him. "I don't want to upset you."

"Honey, you couldn't upset me. Especially with a gift."

"I'm serious, Oscar. This is coming from a pure place in my heart. Please know I care about you."

Well, with a build up like that, now Oscar was nervous himself. He eyed the box. During his FBI career he'd been around more than a few bombs, and he didn't think one ever scared him half as much as this little red-ribboned gift did at the moment.

Suddenly, he didn't want it. He had a feeling that whatever was inside was about to change everything. He liked his life. For the first time since his boys had disowned him, he was finally having hope. "Let's save it for later," he said, thinking maybe he would hide it away and claim it was lost.

His suggestion seemed to empower her decision, and she thrust it in his hands. "No, open it now."

He glanced at her and then at the box. Slowly, he shook it, noting the rattle inside.

"Go on," she said, smiling now. "Open it."

He took in a deep breath and pulled at the ribbon. It untied in one movement. With gentle precision he slid the wrapping open and pushed out the box.

It was white cardboard, the same type as the paste jewelry came in that his boys used to buy their mom.

He removed the lid and stared down at the white pad of cotton.

Cecelia let out a little giggle.

He glanced at her and slowly removed the cotton, half expecting something to jump out at him.

Inside was a pink flamingo. He stared at it, blinking, and then turned a perplexed glance at Cecelia.

"It's a keychain," she said. "Take it out!"

He removed the metal painted ornament from the box and let it swing in the air. His eyebrows rumpled together, and he was so confused he could hardly think to form the question why?

"Okay, so I heard from Georgie, who heard from her best friend Kari that the Flamingo Realty in Brookfield is getting a new real estate agent." Cecelia leaned back, puffed with pride.

"You?" he asked, his throat feeling dry.

"No, Oscar. Someone else. Someone very near and dear to you. Someone who is flying in from Seattle." She rested her hand on his. "Someone you deserve to get to know. Your granddaughter."

Oscar felt faint.

"You've been patient, and you've given everyone space to heal and grow. But it's time to figure out your family. Time to move forward. And, I'll help you do it." Her thumb gently caressed his.

Oscar saw the determination in her eyes, and he believed her. His gut feeling had been right after all. He wondered at his sons— he loved them so and it broke his heart that they would never forgive him. Yet, how could they, after what he had done?

This item in the box was indeed a link to a permanent life change.

Still, secrets run deep. Deeper than he ever imagined.

And he could never have expected the rollercoaster that was waiting for him right around the corner.

And neither could Cecelia.

Not even Peanut had a clue. But out of the three of them, Peanut was the most prepared for the next greatest adventure of their lives.

The End. Oh, Oscar O'Neil. This man has no idea what's about to happen to him! Check out the Flamingo Realty Mysteries to find out what secret is separating his family. Will his sons ever forgive him? And can Peanut save the day?

Mind Your Manors

A Dead Market

Home Strange Home

Duplex Double Trouble

MidCentury Modern Murder

With Killer Views

There are some delicious recipes below, but first…

About CeeCee James

She is a two time USA Today Best Selling mystery author with her hands full with miniature dachshunds and grandkids. Her favorite hobbies besides writing include reading, painting and hiding rocks, crocheting, and making miniatures. Connect with her readers' page on facebook, and follow her on BookBub and Amazon for flash sales and new releases.

And now the fun stuff! Three free recipes!

Aunt Cecelia's Christmas Star Breakfast Bread

1 package active dry yeast

1/4 cup warm water

3/4 cup warm milk

1/4 cup butter, softened

1 egg at room temperature

1/4 tsp vanilla

1/4 cup granulated sugar

pinch of salt

3 1/2 cups all-purpose flour

3/4 cup raspberry jam

Or- 1/2 cup of sugar

1TBS cinnamon mixed the 2 together

3 tbsp butter, melted

1/4 cup powdered sugar

Mix the water and yeast in a small mixing bowl. In a separate mixing bowl, beat butter until it's smooth. Mix in egg, milk, sugar, and salt into the butter until smoothish. Once the yeast and water is foamy, add into the second bowl and continue to mix.

Slowly add flour. Transfer dough to a well-floured surface. Knead it a few minutes or until it becomes smooth and elastic. After kneading, transfer to a greased bowl and cover. Let it rise in a warm place for about an hour or until the dough has doubled in size.

Once dough has risen, divide into four balls. Take the first dough ball and roll it out into an approx. 12" circle. Place on a large sheet pan or pizza stone. Transfer 1/3 of the jam onto the dough (or cinnamon topping) and spread around, leaving 1/2" of space all the way around. Roll out next dough ball and put on top of first. Layer on jam or other topping. Lick your fingers. Repeat with one more dough balls and the remaining jam. With the last dough ball, roll it out and put it on top, but do not cover with jam.

Once the dough and jam have been layered, place a 2" circle (circular cookie cutter) leave a mark in the middle without cutting all the way through. From there, use a knife to slice the dough away from the circular mark, like sun rays. Make16 even cuts.

Take two pieces right next to each other and spin them outward twice. Pinch ends together like the top of a flower petal. Repeat for the remaining strips.

Cover and let rise for about 1 hour. Preheat oven to 375 degrees. Once dough has risen, bake for about 20 minute or until the top start to turn golden brown. Brush with melted butter, and serve warm. Options- sprinkle with powdered sugar or cinnamon and sugar.

YUM!

Oscar's FullBelly Lasagne

1 Italian sausage

2 24oz jarred spaghetti sauce

12 lasagne noodles, cooked according to package instructions— or a little under.

1 egg

1 tsp Italian seasoning.

8 oz. package shredded mozzarella cheese, divided

8 oz. package shredded Gruyere cheese

¾ c. Parmesan cheese

15 oz. container ricotta cheese (1 container)

Make meat sauce by browning sausage, drain, and then mixing into spaghetti sauce.

Boil the noodles. Better to err on undercooking than overcooking. Drain and rinse with cold water.

Preheat oven to 375

In a large bowl combine ricotta, egg, Italian seasoning and parmesan

In one baking pan, cover bottom with 2 cups or so of meat sauce

Layer 3 noodles

Layer 1/3 of ricotta mixture, and 1/3 of shredded cheeses

Layer 3 noodles.

Layer 1/3 of meat sauce

Layer 1/3 of ricotta mixture, and 1/3 of shredded cheeses.

Layer 3 noodles.

Layer 1/3 of ricotta mixture, and 1/3 of shredded cheeses

Top with the remaining noodles and the remaining meat sauce.

Cover with foil and bake for twenty minutes. Remove and top with divided mozzarella cheese. Bake uncovered for another ten to twelve minutes.

Remove lasagne and let it rest for five minutes and then serve!

Delish! And don't make any bets on if it will snow or not. Or make bets because this dish is worth it.

CeeCee James Chicken Pot Pie aka a cheat version of Cecelia's Lunch Special.

This is a favorite around my house, and so easy!

8 chicken thighs

2 cans of creamed chicken soup

1-1/2 cup chopped carrots

3 celery stalks— chopped

1/2 onion chopped fine

1 cup frozen corn

2 cups frozen peas

1 1/2 tsp poultry seasoning

1 can of biscuits

32 oz chicken broth

I like to start with a cast iron pan. Cook chicken and chop or shred. Place in pan. Add cream of chicken soup and chicken broth. Mix well over medium heat. Bring to boil. Turn heat down to simmer. Add all vegetables and seasoning. Simmer for ten minutes. Open biscuit can. Break each biscuit into four to six pieces and drop into the simmering liquid. Gently stir. Add salt and pepper to taste. Cook until thickened, about fifteen to twenty minutes.

I love this meal on cold rainy evenings. To me it's coziness in a pan. Expect no leftovers!

You guys are the best!

Thank you again for joining me for this short story. I can't tell you how much fun I had writing from Oscar's point of view. I laughed a few times as I pulled out memories of my own grandparents.

Oscar has been an interesting character. For much of his life he was a buttoned-up focused FBI agent, with his family coming second. A far second. And he paid the price.

Years later, for a secret reason, his boys disowned him. He tried to pick up the pieces but when his wife passed without any reconciliation, he kind of gave up. The sadness that descended nearly pulled him into the grave.

Then Cecelia took an interest in him. Just as a neighbor, one kind soul caring for another. Just one time reaching out to make sure another was okay.

Sometimes a few words makes a real difference.

And his path changed.

Suddenly, he realized he wasn't alone. In the process, he met Georgie and Frank (Cherry Pie or Die, the Baker Street Mysteries). Slowly he came out of his shell and had hope that someone really did care about him.

But this little flamingo keychain will change his life forever.

One thing that Oscar learned was that hope is a magical tool. One that we all have. Things do change, and if he could say something to you now, he'd say, "You've got this. You are here for a reason. One step at a time, and keep looking up. And the few words you give to someone— they make a difference in that person's life. You make a difference."

Much love and hugs— so grateful for all of you!

More books by CeeCee James

Flamingo Realty Mysteries

Mind Your Manors

A Dead Market

Home Strange Home

Duplex Double Trouble

MidCentury Modern Murder

With Killer Views

Baker Street Mysteries— Join Georgie, amateur sleuth and historical tour guide on her spooky, crazy adventures. As a fun bonus there's free recipes included!

Cherry Pie or Die

Cookies and Scream

Crème Brûlée or Slay

Drizzle of Death

Slash in the Pan

Terror on Top

Oceanside Hotel Cozy Mysteries—Maisie runs a 5 star hotel and thought she'd seen everything. Little did she know. From haunted pirate tales to Hollywood red carpet events, she has a lot to keep her busy.

Booked For Murder

Deadly Reservation

Final Check Out

Fatal Vacancy

Suite Casualty

Angel Lake Cozy Mysteries—Elise comes home to her home town

to lick her wounds after a nasty divorce. Together, with her best friend Lavina, they cook up some crazy mysteries.

The Sweet Taste of Murder

The Bitter Taste of Betrayal

The Sour Taste of Suspicion

The Honeyed Taste of Deception

The Tempting Taste of Danger

The Frosty Taste of Scandal

About CeeCee James

She is a two time USA Today Best Selling mystery author with her hands full with miniature dachshunds and grandkids. Her favorite hobbies besides writing include reading, painting and hiding rocks, crocheting, and making miniatures. Connect with her readers' page on facebook, and follow her on BookBub and Amazon for flash sales and new releases.

Keep in contact with me! If you are in the reader's group, you know how fun it is. Have a great day!

Made in the USA
Middletown, DE
27 December 2019